The Ugly Duckling

Illustration Giuseppe Di Lernia
Original story by Hans Christian Andersen
Retold by Melanie Joyce
Project editor Clare Lloyd
Design assistant Eleanor Bates
Jacket designer Charlotte Jennings
Jacket co-ordinator Issy Walsh
Producer John Casey
Pre-production producer Heather Blagden
Managing editor Penny Smith
Managing art editor Mabel Chan
Creative director Helen Senior
Publishing director Sarah Larter

First published in Great Britain in 2019 by
Dorling Kindersley Limited
80 Strand, London, WC2R 0RL

Copyright © 2019 Dorling Kindersley Limited
A Penguin Random House Company
10 9 8 7 6 5 4 3 2 1
001–313516–July/2019

A CIP catalogue record for this book
is available from the British Library.
ISBN: 978-0-2413-7098-8

Printed and bound in China

A WORLD OF IDEAS:
SEE ALL THERE IS TO KNOW

www.dk.com

Notes for Parents and Carers

Here are some ideas for discussing important themes in *The Ugly Duckling* with young children. Use these notes to prompt discussion during and after reading the book.

- Do you think the ducklings and the farm animals are kind to the ugly duckling? Why do you think they behave in the way they do?

- If you met the ugly duckling how would you treat him? Talk about the importance of being kind to others.

- How does the duckling react when the children try to play with him? Why do you think he responds in this way?

- Talk about how the duckling changes and what he becomes. Do you think he is happy at the end of the story and can you say why?

It was summer in the countryside. By a cool pond near a little farm, a mother duck sat on her nest of eggs.

Suddenly the eggs began to hatch. Cute little yellow ducklings hopped out of their eggshells. Cheep-cheep, quack, quack, they went, flapping their tiny wings.

Before long there was just one egg left in the nest. It was much larger than the others. At last it began to crack.

A big fluffy shape appeared. "What an ugly duckling," said one of the little yellow ducklings.

"Honk! Honk!" went the ugly duckling.

"It can't quack!" laughed another yellow duckling.

They laughed even harder when the clumsy duckling tripped and fell over its own feet.

One by one the baby ducks splashed into the water behind their mother. The ugly duckling swam at the back.

The mother duck loved each and every one of her ducklings — including the big fluffy one.

The mother duck took her brood up to the farmyard. The animals adored the cute little ducklings, but they didn't like the big fluffy one.

They pecked and nipped him. "You're ugly!" they cried. The duckling was so upset, he ran away as fast as he could.

He came to a cottage where a cat and a hen lived with an old woman.

"Purr like me and you can stay," said the cat.

"You can stay if you lay eggs," said the hen.

The duckling couldn't purr or lay eggs,
so he left the cottage.

The duckling felt very lonely.
Autumn arrived and one
evening he saw graceful white
birds flying high above.
He longed to be like them.

But as the weather grew cold, the waters froze.
Soon the ugly duckling was stuck fast in ice!

A kind man rescued the shivering duckling and took him home to show his children.

The children wanted to play and chased the duckling. He was so frightened that he toppled the milk bucket and fled back outside into the snow.

It was a long hard winter for the poor duckling.
The freezing days and nights seemed to last forever.

Then one day the sun began to shine.
Warm sunbeams melted the ice.

A lark sang because spring had come. The ugly duckling noticed three beautiful birds had landed on the water. They were the same ones he had seen in the autumn.

He felt sure the birds would be mean, but he
was not afraid anymore.

The ugly duckling did not fly away when the birds spotted him hiding in the bulrushes. To his surprise, they were friendly and welcoming.

He swam out from his hiding place and looked at his reflection in the water. He had changed!

He was no longer an ugly duckling, but
a brave and magnificent swan!

The older swans bowed their heads to their new friend. He rustled his feathers and curved his slender neck.

He was filled with joy when little children pointed and cried out, "Look at that lovely new swan!"

In a flurry of wings the young swan flew off
with his new flock. He had never dreamed of
such happiness when he was an ugly duckling
and knew he would never be lonely again.